HO HO HO

NO PART OF THIS PUBLICATION MAY BE REPRODUCED, STORED IN A RETRIEVAL SYSTEM OR TRANSMITTED IN ANY FORM OR BY ANY MEANS, ELECTRONIC, MECHANICAL, PHOTOCOPYING, RECORDING OR OTHERWISE WITHOUT WRITTEN PERMISSION OF THE PUBLISHER. FOR INFO REGARDING PERMISSION WRITE TO LETTER H PUBLISHING, 125 TWIN LAKES DR. FAIRFIELD OH - SANTA'S WATCHING

ISBN-13: 978-0692336304

ISBN-10: 0692336303

P.S. - TEXT AND ILLUSTRATIONS COPYRIGHT  MS HEATHER 2014

FORMATTED BY ONE OF SANTA'S ELVES
- ROSEMARIE GILLEN -
HHtp://www.rosemariegillen.com

I0540101

To: Princess LookingGlass

MY COLLEGE ROOMMATE WHO ABSOLUTELY WOULD NOT LET ME PLAY CHRISTMAS MUSIC IN OUR APARTMENT UNTIL THE DAY AFTER THANKSGIVING! AND TO ANYBODY ELSE WHO LOVES CHRISTMAS AS MUCH AS I LOVE IT!

NOTE

STAY ON THE NICE LIST AND CHECK OUT THESE OTHER BOOKS BY MISS HEATHER

✳ Surfer Dude
✳ Hockey Dude
and coming soon... Rocker Dude!

STOP BY & SAY HI

MISSHEATHERSSTORYTIME.COM
AND/OR
Miss Heather's Storytime on Facebook ♡♥

ANOTHER NOTE

I MADE A LITTLE LIST THE OTHER DAY

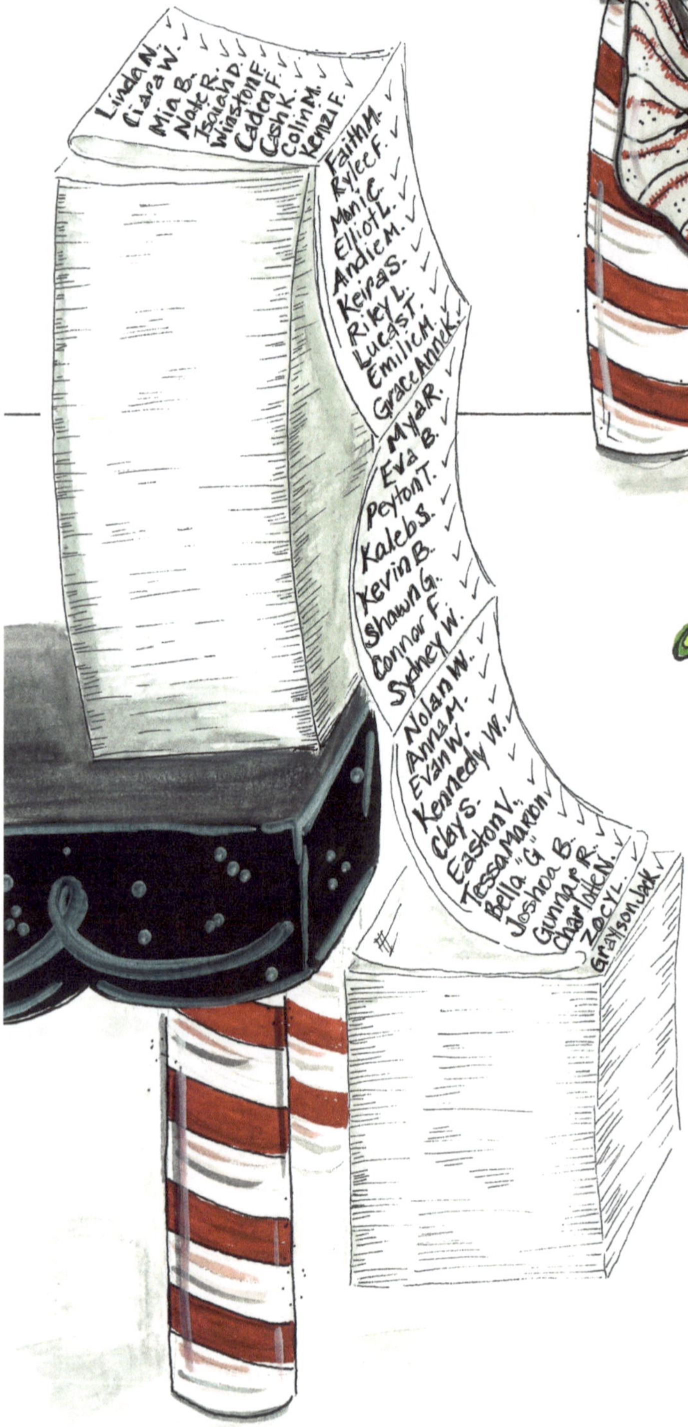

I CHECKED IT

TWICE

- AND -

WENT ON MY WAY.

WHEN I

SAW THE CALENDAR ON THE WALL

I REALIZED I DIDN'T

HAVE MUCH TIME AT ALL!

THANK GOODNESS Mrs. Claus

HAD MADE A LIST TOO —

OF ALL OF THE THINGS
I STILL NEEDED
TO DO!

MY **R**EINDEER TO FEED.

THEN TO THE POST OFFICE —
MY MAIL TO READ.

LETTERS FROM **N**ORWAY,

BRAZIL AND PERU,

FROM AFRICA, ENGLAND

AND MAYBE FROM

YOU!

NOW CHECK ON THE ELVES WHO ARE MAKING THE TOYS-

The ones I will deliver to: Good girls and boys.

THEN
I FINISHED
THE LIST MRS. "C"
MADE FOR ME
BY HEADING BACK HOME
WITH THEE PERFECT TREE

"WHAT IS SO FUNNY?
DID YOU HEAR A GOOD JOKE"?

STILL GIGGLING, SHE STOOD
AND GAVE MY BELLY A POKE!

I SET DOWN THE TREE
TO TAKE A GOOD LOOK

THEN I STARTED TO LAUGH 'TIL
MY BIG BELLY SHOOK.

WE LAUGHED 'TIL WE CRIED,

THE MRS. AND I,

(I S'POSE BY NOW YOU'RE WONDERING WHY) ???

WELL—
SOMEWHERE,
SOMEHOW...

MY SWEATER
-GOT CAUGHT-

ON THE PATH I HAD TRAVELLED—

And behind me MOST of it HAD completely UNraveled.

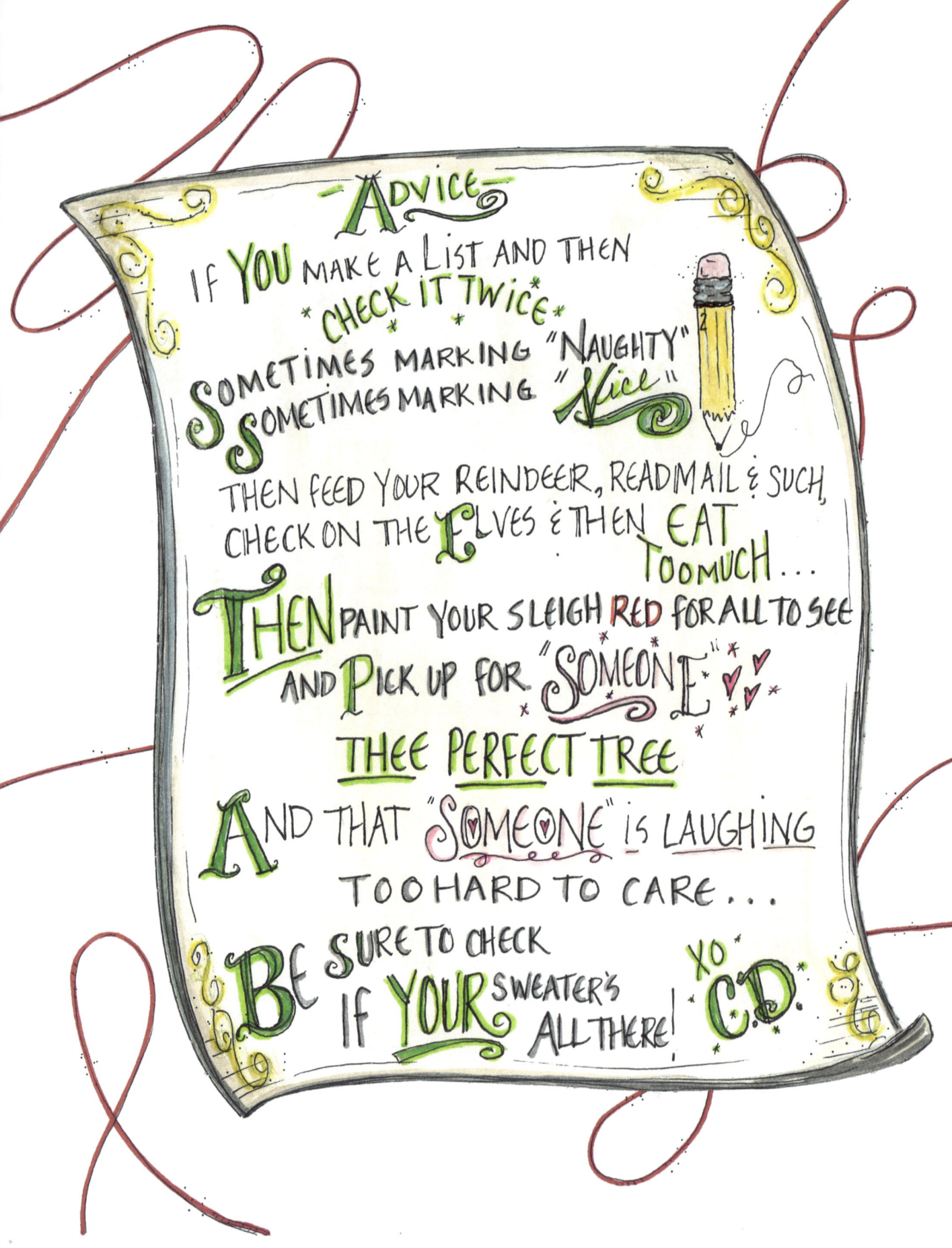

THE END...

─OF MY SWEATER THAT IS!!

www.ingramcontent.com/pod-product-compliance
Lightning Source LLC
Chambersburg PA
CBHW041009170626
46815CB00002B/226